The Servant
of
Souls

Dragon Riders of Osnen Book 8

RICHARD FIERCE

Dragonfire Press

Copyright © 2020 Richard Fierce

Cover design by germancreative.

Cover art by Rosauro Ugang

ISBN: 978-1-947329-51-5

CONTENTS

1

I stared up at the mountain that towered over the surrounding peaks.

It seemed higher than I remembered. The pinnacle was lost in the clouds above, and somewhere up there on a plateau was Valgaard. I shivered just thinking about the thick snow that blanketed the crags.

"Did we have to come here first?" I complained.

"I'd rather not have come here at all," Maren replied, "but we need to explore every avenue, and Valgaard is the closest school."

"I know," I muttered. I knelt and rolled up my bedroll, tying the thin cords on the ends to secure it, and placed it in Sion's saddle. "I just hate the cold. And Hrodin. Mostly Hrodin."

Maren smiled playfully and shook her head. "We'll make this quick and painless," she said. "Like pulling off a bandage."

That didn't change my dread about going.

How are you feeling? I asked Sion, walking around to her head.

Warm, she replied. *I remember the coldness of this place. It was not pleasant.*

Yes, but their stables were comfortable.

Sion snorted, and I could tell by the disdain in

the bond that she was not happy. I rubbed the scales along her neck and she hummed contentedly.

As Maren said, we'll be in and out in no time.

Let us hope so, Sion said.

"Are you two ready?" Maren asked.

"Yes."

I climbed up Sion's shoulder and settled into the saddle. The fur cloak I'd brought from the Citadel was stuffed into a large pocket on the saddle, and I debated with myself about putting it on now. I glanced at the sky. It was midday and warm, so I decided to wait.

"If you feel anything wrong with the bond, land immediately," Maren said. "It doesn't matter where, as long as you can do so safely."

I nodded, though I was hoping we didn't run into that problem. Given the way things had gone the last few weeks, I knew that was a stretch.

Tell me if you feel any sign of weakness, I said.

I will.

Sion hunched down and positioned her legs, then jumped. Her wings stretched out and she flapped, soaring vertically. I leaned forward and braced myself against her, holding on tightly. She climbed higher and higher until the ground below was hardly recognizable. Once Sion leveled out, I eased my grip on the saddle and looked for Demris.

He and Maren weren't far behind. With a couple of flaps, he caught up to us and flew beside Sion.

We continued our ascent, but in gradual circles around the mountain. The air began to thin, and I could see giant puffs of air escaping from Sion's nostrils. The temperature steadily dropped, and I was forced to retrieve the fur cloak. I wrapped it around myself and rubbed my hands together, occasionally blowing my hot breath onto them.

There's a storm brewing, Sion said.

I looked around, but it was difficult to tell where it was. We were among the clouds, and everything was veiled in a thin misty fog. The cold was becoming unbearable, and my eyes were dry. I pulled the cloak tighter around me, but the wind and the cold still nipped at my flesh. I didn't think I could feel more miserable, and I was wrong.

The storm struck, sudden and fierce.

I felt Sion tense against the wind, and it jostled her about wildly. The cold intensified, hitting me like a physical blow, and I shivered uncontrollably.

"We're close!"

Maren shouted the words, though I barely heard them. Her voice was drowned away by the thrashing wind. She pointed to the right, but I couldn't see anything through the fog and the snow.

Can you see it? I asked Sion.

Yes, she replied. *It's not far, but this wind is making it tough to maneuver.*

Just do your best, I said.

I always do.

You're starting to sound like Maren. I flooded the bond with mirth.

Sion rumbled in reply. I felt her body tilt as she tried to angle herself toward Valgaard. A powerful gust of wind struck me, pushing me backward in the saddle. I grunted and leaned far forward, practically lying on Sion to keep from being ripped from the saddle. The wind screeched. I blinked away flakes of snow and my heart fell into my stomach. That wasn't the wind.

It was Maren.

Demris was spiraling down, his wings limp and useless. Before I could alert Sion, Demris struck the side of the mountain, disappearing in a mound of snow.

Demris just fell!

Without warning, Sion dived. Her head snaked back and forth.

There! I shouted, trying to project the image of where he'd landed. It was fragmented, but Sion discerned the location. She tucked her wings in as she neared the spot and we landed roughly, her claws scrabbling against the stone outcropping that jutted out from the mountain. I jumped down off of her back and pushed myself through knee-high snow.

There was a shallow cave, and I spotted green scales mingled against the white powdery snow. I reached him and started shoveling the snow off with my hands. Sion joined me, and she used her tail to scoop large piles away. It felt like an eternity before we uncovered him. He was lying on his right side, which meant Maren was probably in the cave.

I carefully climbed over Demris and saw Maren. Thankfully, she wasn't under Demris, but she was clutching her leg.

"Are you all right?" I studied her limb. It didn't look broken, but I wasn't a healer.

"It hurts here," Maren said, pointing at her shin. "It's burning like fire."

"Do you think it's broke?"

"No," Maren shook her head. "But I don't think I can walk on it."

"Sion can't lift Demris, and I can't carry you up the mountain in this weather."

We stared at each other in silence.

"I'll get help," I finally said. "Sion can stay here with you, and I'll go to Valgaard."

"Are you sure you can make it?"

"I have to try. We can't stay here. Demris will freeze to death."

Maren looked past me to stare at him. She nodded.

"I'll be back as soon as possible," I said. "Stay here in the cave."

I crawled over Demris and looked up the mountain. The storm was raging, but I could see the edge of the plateau where Valgaard was situated.

I need you to watch over Demris and Maren, I said to Sion. *I'm going to get help.*

We could fly, but I don't think I could make it into the air without crashing into the mountain. The wind is too strong.

I don't want to risk it, I replied. *Try to keep them warm. I'll return with help.*

Sion nuzzled me. I ran my frozen hands along her snout, brushing some snow off. The feeling was gone from my fingers. They were pale and tinged blue, and I could barely move them. I turned away from Sion and looked for the easiest way to climb up. With everything covered in snow, it was hard to tell. Part of the cliff face had several lumps sticking out. I cleared the snow off one and realized they were large stones embedded in the soil.

I clenched and released my hands a few times, trying to work the circulation back into my fingers, then started scaling the wall. I'd barely made any progress when I realized how terrible my idea was. Granted, there wasn't another option, but climbing a mountain in the middle of a snowstorm was akin to putting out a fire with air.

The rocks were jagged and cut into my hands, but I continued climbing. The longer Demris was unconscious, the quicker the cold would take his life. After all we'd gone through to bring him back from the Island of Lost Souls, I couldn't allow him to die again. I reached the top of the cliff face, but it was a small victory. Valgaard was still high above. At least I could walk along the slopes now and give my hands a rest.

There was a natural path, though there was no sign that anyone used it. I trudged along, the path progressively inclining until it stopped at a wall of rocks. They weren't completely covered in snow, and the climb was slightly easier. Again, I reached the top and found another natural trail that led up toward the plateau.

The storm had calmed, but the snow was still falling heavily. I stopped for a moment to shake the snow off my cloak, then continued. Every inch of my body was freezing, and I was pretty sure some snow had gotten into my boots and melted. I continuously reminded myself that things could be worse, which was probably why they ended up that way.

A throaty growl filled the air and I stopped in my tracks. It didn't sound like a dragon, so it likely wasn't a scout from the school. I slowly moved my head and looked for the source of the sound, but I didn't see anything. Time was wasting away, so I started walking again. There was a blur of movement above me to my left and I stopped. I saw it now.

It was a mountain cat.

2

The cat watched me intently, and I knew that it considered me an intruder, if not its prey.

It was roughly three feet in length, not including its bushy tail, and thick with muscle. The head was domed, and its muzzle was short. Its fur was mostly white, blending in with the surroundings, and its face was dotted with small black spots. I'd never seen anything like it before.

It growled again and hunched down, preparing to spring at me. I tried to draw my sword, but the blade was trapped in the sheath. I kept yanking on the hilt, and I suspected the cold had frozen it stuck. I quickly unhooked the belt and gripped the handle, swinging the entire thing up as I took a defensive stance.

The numbness in my hands made it difficult to hold the sword steady, and when the giant cat pounced and knocked me down, I lost my grip on the hilt and dropped the weapon. The cat snarled and hissed as it tried to claw me. Despite its small size, it was extremely ferocious. I brought my left arm up to block my face, and the cat latched its sharp teeth onto my bracer. It pulled and jerked, causing my wound to flare with pain.

Eldwin? Sion's voice filled my mind.

I mentally closed off the bond so I could focus. I clenched my right hand into a fist and struck the cat in the head. The blow sent pain shooting through my numb fingers, and I cried out involuntarily. The animal seemed surprised that I fought back. I punched it again. And again. The fourth blow made the cat release my arm. It leaped off of me and bounded away, traveling up the mountainside.

My entire body was shivering now, but I wasn't sure if it was from the cold. The cat had nearly ripped my arm from the socket. I struggled to my feet and saw fresh blood had stained the snow. The bandage that covered my wound was soiled. Muttering under my breath, I retrieved my sword and wrapped the belt around my waist. I incessantly looked to where the cat had fled, but it didn't return.

I continued along the trail that sloped up toward the plateau. My teeth chattered uncontrollably, despite my attempt to clench my jaw shut, and the cold seeped into every part of my being. The cloak did little to warm me, and eventually, I quit trying to keep myself wrapped up in it.

The natural path crested a hill, and I thought I glimpsed the walls of Valgaard before my legs gave out on me. I staggered and fell, face-planting into a mound of snow. My mind had told my arms to break my fall, but they had refused to obey. I didn't both trying to get up. Everything hurt. Every muscle begged for rest. I knew I was almost there, but I convinced myself that a short break would help. That was the last coherent thought before everything went dark.

I became aware that I was moving. Or rather, someone was moving me. I forced my eyes open.

Through blurred vision, I saw that someone tall and muscular was lifting me from the snow. His armor was made of leather and covered with fur, which felt warm against my face as he easily tossed me over his shoulder. I flitted in and out of consciousness until something pungent filled my nose.

"Oh, gods," I mumbled, turning my head away from the smell.

"He lives," a deep voice said. "Tell Master Hrodin."

I heard footsteps as someone left, followed by a door closing.

"Can you hear me?" the voice asked.

"Yes," I replied, cracking my eyes open. A familiar face stared down at me, though I couldn't remember his name. It seemed an eternity had passed since I'd last seen him. "I'm Eldwin."

"I remember," the man replied. "I am Kell."

Kell. That's what it was.

"I need help." I sat up with a groan, every inch of my body screaming at me to stay down.

"You are safe," Kell said. "Where are the dragons? I saw two before they disappeared in the storm."

"That's why I need help. My friend's dragon got ill and fell. He's unconscious, and my friend is hurt. We need to help them before they freeze to death."

"Be still," Kell admonished. "You'll open the

wound again."

I glanced around and noticed we were in a small chamber that appeared to serve as an infirmary. It was clean, but it seemed unused. The door opened and another man entered, but it wasn't Hrodin. He ignored me and spoke to Kell in another language. Kell responded, and the man left again.

"What was that about?" I asked.

"He said Master Hrodin and Skarmundr are going down to get your friend."

"I need to go with him." I tried to slide off the table I was on, but Kell stopped me.

"You need to rest," he said. "Master Hrodin will take care of them."

I wanted to be stubborn and argue, but my exhaustion stole what little energy I had left. I nodded and laid back down, intending to rest my muscles. Although the table wasn't comfortable, I ended up dozing off. My eyes snapped open when I heard the door open again, and this time it was Hrodin who entered. He was carrying Maren, and he set her down on a table across from me.

"Check her leg," he ordered Kell.

Kell walked over to Maren and touched her injured leg in various spots. Maren winced a few times, but otherwise, she kept a stoic expression on her face.

"It's not broken," Kell confirmed.

"That's good news," I said. "What of our

dragons? Where are they?"

"They are in the stable," Hrodin answered. "Skarmundr had to carry the green one."

Hrodin was a big man, standing nearly seven feet in height. He wore a steel breastplate decorated with the head of a dragon, and a thick black wolf's pelt draped his shoulder, stretching down to his ankles. The men of Valgaard were monstrous in size compared to the men of Osnen, and they were made of hardier stuff. I couldn't imagine living in Valgaard with the constant snow and bone-chilling cold weather.

"I assume you both are here for a reason," Hrodin said. "We will talk tonight at the feast."

"A feast?" Kell asked, an edge of excitement in his tone.

"Yes. The feast is in honor of our guests, heroes of the battle against the False King."

"We are honored," Maren said.

"Show them to the guest quarters," Hrodin said to Kell. "Use the hot baths and get some rest. Our feasts last long into the night."

"Thank you, Master Hrodin," I said.

He nodded, then left us with Kell. The big man smiled. "I love feasts. Come, I will show you to your room. Can you walk?" he asked Maren.

"I can try," Maren replied. She rose from the table and paused briefly before putting her weight on her injured leg. Her limb tremored and she leaned against the table. "I don't think it's wise just yet."

"No matter," Kell said. "I can carry you."

I slid off my table with the intent of offering to carry her instead, but I quickly realized there was no way I was going to be able to in my current state. Before Maren could argue, Kell scooped her up and carried her to the door. He glanced over his shoulder at me, and I followed after him.

"Do I need to carry you also?" Kell asked.

Maren giggled.

"No, thank you," I replied. "I can manage."

I opened the door, and Kell led the way out, navigating us along the hallways to a stairway that led up to the second floor of the school. There were two wings, one to the left and the right. Kell took us down the right wing, all the way to the last door. Our time here previously was a bit muddled in my head, and I couldn't remember what rooms we'd stayed in.

Kell shifted Maren to one arm and pushed the door open with the other, then stepped inside and set Maren down on the edge of the bed.

"The bathing chamber is at the other wing," Kell said. "The students cleaned the tubs and refilled them earlier, so you can enjoy them in peace. I'll come and get you when the feast is ready."

"Thank you," I said.

Kell left, closing the door behind him. I sat beside Maren on the bed and tucked a few stray hairs behind her ear.

"I'm sorry I left you behind," I said.

"Don't be sorry," Maren replied. "It's because of you we were rescued by Hrodin."

"I felt guilty for leaving as soon as I stepped away from the cave. It was the only option I could think of."

"And it worked out."

"Barely. I almost got eaten by a mountain cat before I collapsed in the snow."

Maren's brow rose curiously. "I've got to hear this."

3

After I related my near-death experience, Maren and I left the room and wandered down to the other wing to find the bathing chamber. A hint of familiarity washed over me as we entered the room. Steam rose from the water that filled the tubs, adding a feeling of serenity to the atmosphere. It was a jarring difference from the landscape outside.

I helped Maren to one of the tubs and averted my gaze so she could undress. There was a quiet splash, followed by a contented groan.

"The water feels great," Maren said.

"I wonder how they keep the water warm once they fill the tubs?"

"With magic," she replied.

I turned around to look at her. The tubs weren't very tall, maybe three feet, but they rested atop stones that lifted them a foot off the ground. A wooden step stool provided the way up to climb in. I was tempted to peek at Maren's intimate areas, but I managed to avoid doing so by walking over to another tub. My face flushed with embarrassment.

"If they are using magic for things like this, it seems unlikely that they are feeling the effects we are," I said, pulling my boots off. I stripped my clothes off, careful not to jostle my wound too much, and climbed into the tub. The warm water pushed away the chill. I set my left arm on the edge of the tub, not wanting to get the new bandage wet.

"The magic here feels different," Maren said slowly. It sounded like a realization to her.

"How so?"

"I'm … not sure. The difference is subtle, but it's there. It doesn't seem to be as weak, either, but it *is* being affected."

"Maybe they haven't noticed yet," I said.

"We'll find out soon enough."

We relaxed in the water for a long while. I opened the bond and felt Sion's presence. She was sleeping, but her mind stirred when she felt me.

Just checking on you, I said.

She hummed in reply, and I withdrew but left the bond open. Once my skin began to wrinkle, I decided to get out of the tub. I dried myself with a long cloth and got dressed, then kept my back to Maren while I waited on her.

After she was proper, we walked together back to our room. She put most of her weight on me as her leg was still hurting her, but I didn't mind. The bath had worked the tension out of my muscles, and aside from the pain of my wound, I felt a lot better.

Maren laid on the bed and quickly fell asleep. I wasn't tired, so I contented myself with lying beside her. She seemed so much more at peace when she slept. When she was awake, she was always thinking, always trying to figure out how to fix things. She was the most beautiful woman I knew, inside and out. Perhaps one day we would life-bond, but for now, I was happy with the way things were between us.

I was lost in my thoughts and hadn't realized how much time had passed until there was a knock at the door. I gently slid out of the bed and opened the door to find Kell.

"The feast is beginning," he said. He held out a worn staff. "This is for Maren. She can use it to help her walk."

I accepted the staff and turned around to see Maren was awake. She rubbed her eyes and smiled at me. "Time for food?"

"Yes," I replied. I walked over and gave her the staff. "Kell said this should help you with walking."

Maren looked past me and waved at Kell. "Thank you!"

She rose from the bed and gripped the staff with both hands, then slowly stepped toward the door. She adjusted her hands, then stepped again. She reminded me of an elderly person that needed assistance to move around, and I smiled to myself. She quickly got the hang of using the staff, and we followed Kell along the hall and down the stairway.

At the bottom of the stairs, we turned right and headed past the throne room. On top of being master of the school, Hrodin fashioned himself a king after his descendants. The first time we'd met him, he'd been just as pompous as any other noble I'd encountered. Ahead, music drifted on the air, echoing off the stone walls of the school.

We entered a large chamber full of people. They were all dressed similarly to Kell, with leather armor and fur pelts. The music was coming from a group of men playing trumpet-like instruments in a corner. The instruments were made of wood that had been split lengthwise, the interior hollowed, and the two halves were banded back together tightly with various lengths of willow bands.

"What are those?" I asked Kell.

"They play the lur," he replied. "It's our most popular instrument."

The long wooden apparatus looked odd, but the sound they produced was pleasant. I turned my attention to the long table that stretched down the center of the room. When Hrodin had said he was throwing a feast, he wasn't exaggerating. There were dozens of various plates of meat, including fish, as well as fresh bread, wheels of cheese, fruits, berries, and several other dishes I didn't recognize.

I wondered how they had some of the items, considering there was no farming land anywhere near the school. Kell directed us to chairs a few spaces down from Hrodin, who raised a drinking horn in the air when he saw us. He seemed friendlier than I remembered, but he'd probably had a decent amount to drink already, which would explain the change. Between the music and the loud conversations, the room was full of boisterous noise.

"Quiet down!" Hrodin shouted.

Nobody paid him any heed, so he slammed his giant fist down onto the table.

"Silence!" he demanded.

The room went quiet, and even the music stopped. Hrodin stood, still holding his drinking horn.

"We have two guests with us that we are here to honor," his deep voice boomed. "Eldwin Baines and Maren Toft. They were at the battle against the False King with me, and I vouch for their prowess." He lifted his horn, and everyone at the table did the same. "We salute you."

"We salute you!" A chorus of voices repeated.

"Thank you," Maren said, offering a bow of her head to Hrodin. I followed her example, but I found it curious he was honoring us for an old deed. Had he not heard about the things Maren and I and done to stop Demris when he was ravaging the Terranese cities? I supposed it was possible that Anesko hadn't shared that information with him.

"I remember the day well," Hrodin said as he sat back down. "The Necromancer and his undead dragon were wreaking havoc among our ranks. Skarmundr and I tried to destroy the dracolich, but it was a powerful adversary controlled by dark magic. These two pierced its heart, providing a way to reach the False King's fortress."

Murmurs of appreciation rose from those present. His retelling wasn't wrong, but it had been much more harrowing than he implied.

"Tell us how you cut the False King's head off," someone said.

Hrodin smiled. "After I cut down the Necromancer, I went inside the castle to find the False King. He was a coward, hiding like a frightened child. He tried to flee, but I trapped him. With a single swing of my blade, I removed his head from his body. Dark magic or not, no one survives something like that."

A cheer arose, and people began chanting "Hrodin! Hrodin!"

He basked in their adulation for a moment, then raised his hand for silence.

"We are not here to admire me, but our guests. Let us eat and drink to honor their deeds and their names."

With that, everyone began to fill their plates and drink from their horns. From the other side of the table, Kell set a horn in front of me.

"This is a gift for you," he said.

"Thank you," I replied. "I'm grateful to receive it."

Kell looked at Maren and placed one in front of her as well. It was more decorative than mine, ornamented with gold and silver filigree. It had to be worth a small fortune. Maren seemed more surprised than I was.

"Thank you," she said softly, holding the horn up to regard the beauty of the metalwork.

We ate and drank, all while listening to the conversations around us. Nobody spoke of the issues we were seeing in Osnen, and I began to suspect that although Maren said the magic here was being affected, Hrodin and the others hadn't noticed yet. As the night went on, and the ale flowed, Hrodin became even more welcoming.

"Tell me," he said. "What has brought you to my domain?"

Maren and I exchanged looks, and I nodded at her. She cleared her throat and looked at Hrodin.

"We've come to see if you've noticed anything happening to magic or to your bonds. In Osnen, something is causing our spells to fail and our dragons to become ill."

Hrodin tilted his head to the side and ran a hand over his beard. "No," he replied. "There is nothing like that happening here."

"How certain are you?" Maren asked.

"Completely," Hrodin replied.

Maren shrugged. "Perhaps whatever is causing it has not reached you yet."

"Perhaps," Hrodin said. "Or perhaps the people of Osnen are weaker than we are, and we won't be affected at all."

I rolled my eyes. Maren didn't say anything, but I was confident she was biting back a harsh reply. It seemed we had come here for nothing. At least, nothing that would help us.

"What is new here?" I asked, changing the subject. "Have you taken in new students?"

"A few," Hrodin answered. "We don't have many dragons that are bondless, so we must wait for hatchlings. There are a few eggs whose time is almost upon us."

My curiosity was piqued. I'd never seen a dragon egg before. "Can we see them?" I asked.

"The eggs?" Hrodin asked, scrunching his face.

"Yes."

He seemed confused by the request but nodded. "Yes. They are in the stable where it is warm. I will take you there after the feast."

I was excited to see what they looked like, and I almost missed it when Hrodin said something about a wedding.

"You're getting married?" I asked. "To who?"

Hrodin smiled and looked at Maren. "To her."

4

Not this again.

"I'm sorry? I don't understand," I said.

"We had an arrangement," Hrodin replied. "In exchange for my aid against the False King, Maren agreed to marry me."

"Yes, and you rescinded that arrangement when Demris was killed," Maren said. "I believe your letter said you couldn't marry someone who didn't have a dragon."

"I did," Hrodin confirmed. "And yet, now you have your dragon back. That's a tale I'd like to hear one day." He took a drink from his horn, tilting the thing too much, and ale sloshed down his beard. It was apparent that he'd had much to drink.

"He's drunk," I whispered to Maren. "I think he's just talking nonsense."

"Let us hope so," she whispered back.

The feast carried on late into the evening, just as Hrodin had said it would. As I watched the others partake of the food and ale, I decided that they were a gluttonous lot. People began to pass out at the table. My eyes were getting heavy, and I decided it was time to turn in for the night. I patted Maren's thigh and she turned to me, her eyes bleary.

"I think I'm going to head up to the room," I said.

"I'm coming, too," Maren replied. "I've been dozing off for a while now."

I rose from my chair and offered Maren my hand. Hrodin watched us, his eyes blinking more times than I thought was necessary.

"Did you still want to see the eggs?" he asked.

Maren took my hand and stood, then grabbed her staff and steadied herself. I had almost forgotten about the eggs. My exhaustion was no match for my curiosity.

"Yes, I do," I answered.

"So do I," Maren said.

Hrodin nodded tiredly. He struggled up from his chair and grabbed his drinking horn, motioning to Kell.

"Come with us," he said.

If Kell had drunk as much ale as Hrodin, he certainly handled it better. The big man stood and aided Hrodin with walking in a straight line. Maren and I followed them, and although her pace was slowed by her injury, we were able to keep up with them due to Hrodin's clumsy ambling.

We exited the castle and I immediately regretted the decision. The snow had continued to fall, and a bitter wind cut through my clothes. I tried to shield Maren from the wind by pulling her close, but she hissed in a breath every time a gust whipped around us. Her staff kept getting stuck in the snow, even with Hrodin and Kell creating a path ahead of us.

Although the stable wasn't far from the castle, the weather made the short trek miserable.

The stable was a large cave behind the castle, set into the mountainside. We stepped across the threshold of the entrance and warmth immediately pushed the chill away. I remembered from our last visit that the cave was magically warmed. Unlike last time, there were no other dragons present. Among the first row of grottos, I spotted Sion and Demris. Their heads stuck out of the smaller caves, and Demris perked up when he saw Maren. She hobbled awkwardly over to him and embraced him, settings her staff aside.

How is Demris feeling? I asked Sion.

He is better. I feared he might have broken a wing, but he didn't sustain any injuries other than to his pride. He didn't appreciate being carried by another dragon.

I smiled as I envisioned what that must have looked like.

At least he's all right, I replied. *It could have been worse. Are there any other dragons in here? I don't see any if there are.*

No, Sion answered. *The big white one brought Demris here, then he left.*

His name is Skarmundr. He's Hrodin's dragon.

Yes, I know. He's just as arrogant as his bonded, too.

That's not surprising, I said.

Hrodin went into a fit of coughing, having choked on his ale while drinking from his horn. Once he recovered, he wiped his mouth with the back of his hand.

"Come," he said. "The eggs are this way."

To the right was a passageway that led into an adjoining cave. It was smaller than the first one but still massive in size. A large fire burned within a ring of stones, and three large smooth white rocks were spaced around it. Hrodin walked over to one of the rocks and ran his hand along the side of it.

"This one will hatch first, I think," he said, slurring his words. He laid his head against it and closed his eyes.

And then I realized that the stones were actually eggs. My eyes widened. They were huge, much bigger than I imagined a dragon egg would be. All three were of similar size, and they towered at least six feet in height. Specks of silver mingled among the white, giving off a glittering effect when the light of the fire hit them just right.

"Can I touch them?" I asked.

"Yes." It was Kell who answered.

I walked to the egg beside Hrodin and gently put my hand on it. It was warm, and I could feel a slight vibration. There was a pattern to it. *Thrum, thrum, thrum.* Pause. *Thrum, thrum, thrum.*

"What is that?" I asked, looking at Kell. "The vibrations, I mean."

"The dragon's heartbeat."

"They're bigger than I expected. Are all dragon eggs this big?"

"No. Whites are the largest of all dragons, and so their eggs are bigger than others. They also take longer to hatch. The one you are touching is a few years old."

"Years?" I repeated incredulously.

Kell nodded, a grin spreading across his lips. "Years."

I looked over at Maren. She was standing next to Hrodin, examining the egg he was leaning against.

"They're beautiful," she said.

"You talk as though you've never seen a dragon egg before," Hrodin muttered.

"I haven't," Maren admitted.

"Neither have I," I said.

"Does your school not allow you to pick the egg of your dragon before they hatch?"

Maren shook her head. "No. The Citadel doesn't have dragon eggs, only dragons old enough to bond with."

Hrodin snorted.

"We allow the chosen rider to touch the egg before it hatches," Kell said. "They also speak to them, so that the dragon recognizes their rider's voice after they hatch. It creates a stronger bond."

"After we are married, we can work to change how the Citadel handles the bonding," Hrodin said.

"We aren't getting married," Maren replied.

"Yes, we are. We had an agreement. I kept my end of the bargain, now it's time for you to do the same."

"You called off the wedding. You can't just wave your hand and make it all happen again."

It was clear to me that Hrodin didn't know that Maren was no longer royalty. Instead of mentioning that, I kept my mouth shut and let Maren handle him. Hrodin lifted his horn and downed what ale remained.

"We *will* be married, princess. There's nothing you can say to dissuade me."

I ground my teeth in anger. Hrodin reminded me of Maren's father. Domineering and egotistical. He thought the world belonged to him, and that he could do as he pleased. Well, he would be highly disappointed when he realized Maren wasn't one to follow orders, let alone rules.

"I'm done talking about this," Maren said firmly.

The silence stretched until it became awkward. Hrodin finally looked at Kell. They shared some sort of unspoken conversation, and then Hrodin headed back the way we'd come.

"I'm retiring for the night," he rumbled.

After he was gone, Maren sighed loudly. "He's

like a broken instrument," she said. "Just keeps playing the same note."

Kell remained expressionless, but I nodded at her. "Tell me about it. I thought we were past all that."

"I could stay here all night," Maren said, rubbing the egg. "But I'm tired."

"We have an early day ahead of us," I reminded her. "The Terranese school is far from here."

Maren groaned. "Don't remind me." She sighed again. "Let's go, then."

Kell took the lead and we left the cave, heading back into the freezing cold. Kell had gone quiet, and I suspected it had something to do with the look Hrodin had given him. A sinking feeling settled in my stomach, and I wasn't sure what to expect, but I knew it couldn't be anything good.

We climbed the stairs, and Maren surprisingly didn't need much assistance. Her skill at walking with the staff had developed quickly.

"Thank you for everything," I said to Kell as we reached the door to our room. "If we don't see you in the morning before we leave, it was nice talking to you again."

Kell grunted in reply. I shrugged and went into the room, closing the door behind me. Before I'd taken three steps, the door clicked. I went back and tried to open it, but it was locked. I knew it!

"Guess who just locked us in?" I asked.

"You're kidding," Maren replied.

"I wish." I shook my head. "I knew Hrodin was going to do something like this."

"Well, we can't stay here. We've got to find out if Katori has seen any problems with the magic or the bonds. And there's also the fact that Anesko doesn't know we're gone."

"I'm sure he knows by now," I said. "But I know what you mean."

I looked around the room for anything we could use to get the door open. The drawers of the dresser and the desk were empty. There were candleholders, which were used to illuminate the room, but I doubted they would be strong enough to pry the door open.

"Can you use your magic?" I asked.

Maren frowned. "No. Remember how I told you it comes in waves? The waves have receded for now."

"Great." I looked around the room again, and my eyes settled on the window. "I have an idea."

"What?"

I pointed. "We'll have to make our own way out. We can use the sheets on the bed like rope and scale down the side of the castle."

Maren nodded slowly. "I think it'll work."

"It's going to have to."

Get ready to fly, I told Sion.

Maren pulled the sheets off the bed and knotted the ends together. I grabbed one of the candleholders and set the candles aside, then drew back and hurled the holder at the window. The metal trinket struck the window, but only caused a minor scratch.

"Try again," Maren said.

I retrieved the holder and threw it harder. This time, the window cracked.

"Again," Maren repeated.

"Do you want to try? I asked.

"No, why?"

I smiled at her.

"Fine, I won't say anything," she huffed.

"Don't act like that. Just get ready to fling the sheet out of the window. I'll be surprised if we don't alert anyone with the noise we're making."

I threw the candleholder again. The window shattered from the impact, shards of glass flying in every direction.

"Go, hurry," I urged Maren. She shuffled to the window and tossed one end of the sheet out, tying the other to a bedpost. I walked to the door and put my ear against it. Thankfully, I didn't hear anything.

I rushed over to the window and grabbed onto the sheet, then lowered myself off the edge. The wind was still blowing, and it whipped the sheet around wildly.

"Climb onto my back," I said.

Maren tossed her staff out and I heard it hit the ground below. She climbed onto the edge, then turned around and lowered herself, slipping her arms around my neck. My muscles burned from the exertion of holding us both in place, but once she was in place, I climbed down, gripping the sheet as tightly as I could so we didn't fall. As soon as I reached the end of the last sheet, I knew we had a problem. We were still several feet above the ground.

"We're going to have to jump," I said.

"See you at the bottom," Maren replied.

Her weight was suddenly gone. I looked down, trying to see if she had landed safely. A shadow stood out against the snow.

"Hurry up," Maren whisper-shouted.

I counted to three and let go. My stomach turned as I dropped, and I hit the snow a moment later. It wasn't as far down as I had thought. We hurried to the stable, but with Maren limping along with her staff, it felt like it took us forever.

We entered the stable to find Sion and Demris waiting for us. We mounted up, and a short moment later, we were speeding through the darkness.

5

It took the better part of two days to cross the border between Osnen and Terran.

Most of that time was spent in the saddle, but we occasionally stopped to allow Sion and Demris to rest their wings. The further we got from Valgaard with no sign of pursuit, the more my worry eased. Hrodin was a dangerous man, and while I did fear the possible repercussions of angering him, we had much bigger things to deal with.

Sion and Demris both seemed to be holding up well, but I was worried that they could get ill at any time. Demris's fall on the mountain had proven that my apprehension wasn't unfounded. Still, walking would have taken weeks, if not a month or more, and that was time we didn't have. I doubted Anesko had made any progress with finding the source of the problem, though not for a lack of trying.

Since there was a risk of Sion and Demris going unconscious in mid-flight, we flew lower than normal in case the worst happened. Thankfully, we were almost to the Terranese school, and neither of our dragons had fallen ill. The landscape below changed subtly from farmlands and cities to forested mountains and tall grassy plains. Unlike Osnen, Terran was a place of untamed beauty.

As we neared the coast, the temperature grew

warmer. It was a welcome difference from Valgaard. The humidity wasn't as bad as I remembered, but I assumed that was due to the changing of the seasons. The harsh grip of summer was fading, and soon it would be autumn.

Temples and small towns dotted the land below us, the design of the structures so foreign and exotic from those in Osnen. Terranese buildings were things of beauty and art, with graceful curves and decorative facades, and the school was no exception.

We made one final stop near a shrine. A golden statue of a wingless dragon stood guard beside a slow-moving river. At the base of the statue, people had left various gifts. There was a multitude of coins, as well as gold and silver trinkets. While Sion and Demris drank from the river, I sat in front of the shrine and admired the items, ignoring my urge to pick them up and examine them. Maren stood beside me, leaning on her staff.

"I wonder why people leave things of value here?" I asked, more to myself than for an answer.

"People come here to pay their respect to the gods or to pray for good fortune," Maren replied. "These gifts are a sign of that respect."

"I assume you learned that in your father's court?"

"Yes." Maren's expression darkened.

"Sorry, I didn't mean to bring him up."

"Don't worry about it," she said.

We remained silent for a while. I knew we needed to continue to the school, but there was a peacefulness that exuded from this place and I didn't want to leave yet. Maren shuffled forward and knelt, placing her staff among the gifts. She whispered something I didn't hear, then rose and wandered over to the river.

I stared at the staff, wondering why she left it there. Obviously, she didn't need it anymore, but was there a reason she offered it as a gift? I stood up and stretched, tilting my head left and right until my neck popped. I was about to leave when I spotted something reflecting off the shrine. I glanced over my shoulder, but there was nothing behind me. Moving closer to the statue, I froze.

A familiar face was staring back at me.

"Tyrval?"

The face smiled, then disappeared. I looked around, expecting the old dragon to reappear in physical form. The seconds ticked by, and nothing happened. When she'd visited me in the past, she'd always spoken to me. Perhaps I'd only imagined it.

"Eldwin!"

I peered around the statue and Maren waved at me. "We're waiting for you, tortoise!"

"I'm coming!"

I took one more glance around the area, then joined the others.

"What were you doing?" Maren asked.

"I thought I saw something, but I'm not sure."

"What was it?"

"Not what, but *who*. I thought I saw Tyrval's face reflected in the statue." Maren stared at me expectantly, and I shrugged. "That was it."

"Do you think it has something to do with what's happening?" she asked.

"It's possible," I admitted. "She smiled at me, then faded away."

"If we don't find anything here, maybe we should go see the Assembly."

Maren's words hung in the air, heavy and suffocating, and Tyrval's words reverberated in my mind hauntingly. *If we have need of you, we will call upon you.* I hoped that seeing her face in the statue was not the summons of the Assembly.

"Let's go," I said, ignoring the bad feeling I had in my stomach.

An hour later, we landed outside the walls of the school. The gates were wide open as usual, and we dismounted and headed through, leaving Sion and Demris to sunbathe in the grassy field. We entered the courtyard to find it empty, which I thought was odd. There were no guards, no students, nothing.

"Maybe everyone is inside?" Maren suggested.

The bad feeling in my stomach intensified, but I nodded and walked with her to the doors of the main building. I tried pulling on the ornate handle, but the door didn't budge.

"It seems the doors are barred from the inside," I said.

"We can check the stable. Wasn't there a way in and out of the school down there?"

"Yes, but I don't remember where it is."

Maren shrugged. "We can try searching for it. We didn't come all this way for nothing."

The courtyard wound around the school to the right, and we made our way to the back of the grounds. Much like the Citadel, the Terranese stable was located underground, though the Citadel's was far simpler to navigate. This stable had been a confusing maze of tunnels. We walked through the entrance, which was a sloping dirt pathway that gradually descended. When it leveled out, there was nothing but darkness ahead.

"The waves of magic haven't happened to return yet, have they?" I asked.

"No. I haven't felt the magic at all since we entered Terran."

"Perfect."

The small amount of light that shone down into the tunnel illuminated a wooden rack built for holding weapons, but the rungs were bare. There were a few torches available, and I grabbed two of them and handed one to Maren. On the ground beside the rack was a large piece of flint. I drew my sword and knelt, awkwardly holding the torch in place as I struck my blade against the flint.

After a few failed attempts, the end of the torch finally caught fire. The resin substance on the torch was dry and brittle, and tiny flaming pieces fell off, slowly spinning down to the ground. I sheathed my sword and held my torch near Maren's, and it lit easily.

The tunnel was tall and wide, large enough for two dragons to walk side by side. I lowered my torch, looking at the ground. Claw marks were scattered all along the dirt, but none of them seemed recent.

"Come on," Maren said, walking past me.

I followed after her, glad that her leg injury had healed enough to allow her to walk normally. The tunnel stretched on for a fair distance, but eventually, we came to a split. Two tunnels forked in different directions. I tried to remember where they led, but my memory failed me.

"We should split up. I'll go left."

"I don't think that's a good idea," I said. "We should stick together."

Maren shrugged. "Fine. Let's go this way, then."

We went left. The tunnel had caves on either side. They appeared to be sleeping quarters for dragons, but nothing was in them. We walked and walked, but there seemed to be no end to the tunnel. It just continued on, and eventually, I stopped walking.

"We should go back," I said. "There's clearly

nothing down this way but empty caves."

Maren turned to face me, the flickering light of the torch causing shadows to dance around her. If it wasn't so creepy down here, I would have found the sight somewhat striking. She looked past me, her brows furrowing.

"Nothing, huh?"

I turned around. The torch pushed back the darkness, illuminating a massive white skull. I let out a cry of surprise and staggered back, tripping and falling hard on my backside. My torch clattered to the ground, echoing eerily off the tunnel walls. I clambered back onto my feet and grabbed the torch, then shined it into the cave.

The skull belonged to a dragon. The rest of its bones were laid out in a jumble behind it. Judging by the lack of skin or muscle, the dragon had died a while ago. I turned to Maren.

"As much as I'd like to know what happened, I think we should get aboveground."

Surprisingly, Maren didn't argue with me. She nodded mutely, and I led the way back to the main tunnel. Something terrible had happened here. Where were Katori and the others? Why did the place seem abandoned? A flood of questions filled my mind as we trekked back up to the surface.

I reached the top first and turned around to wait for Maren. She came into view and shouted a warning, but I wasn't quick enough. Something slammed into me, knocking me down. I dropped the torch and rolled onto my back, just in time to see a curved blade hovering inches in front of my face.

6

"The penalty for stealing is death."

The person at the other end of the sword was an intimidating sight and reminded me of Domori. He wore a red cuirass made of steel, with leather plates that hung from the front that offered protection to his lower body and upper legs. Large rectangular leather plates adorned his shoulders, and his thigh guards were made of cloth and leather plates of varying sizes, each one connected to the other with small chains that had been sewn into the cloth. His helmet had a dozen or more iron plates riveted together which included a lacquered metal face mask painted black and red with the twisted visage of a fearsome creature.

"We're not stealing," Maren called out, holding her hands up in the air. "We're riders from Osnen."

I noticed the man with the sword pointed at me wasn't alone. Two others stood behind him, their swords also drawn. One of them wore similar armor, but the mask was different. The third person looked like a woman, though it was hard to tell because long black hair covered their face.

"Riders?" The third figure was definitely female. Her voice was melodic, despite her rough appearance. She stepped around the lead man, using her right hand to brush the hair back from her face.

"Katori?"

It looked like her. Sort of. There was a wild almost fearful look in her eyes as if she was haunted by something. She'd always been thin and small in stature, but now she was also bony and pale. If I didn't know any better, I could have mistaken her for a corpse.

"Do I know you?"

"It's me, Eldwin."

"Eldwin." The way Katori spoke my name was like music, her accent unique and wonderful. Realization dawned on her face. "Eldwin!"

She pushed away the sword that was pointed at my face and offered me her hand. I accepted it and she helped me to my feet.

"I apologize for the rude treatment, but things are not as they once were."

"I see that. What happened here?"

"Come inside," Katori bade, glancing around uneasily. "There is much to tell."

She led us around to the front of the school, and we stopped at the main doors. Katori touched the frame on the right side of the door and ran her finger in a sweeping motion. There was a clicking sound, and she pulled the doors open.

"Magic?" I asked, surprised that it worked.

"No, but maybe to the untrained eye," Katori said.

We went inside and followed her down a long hall. I distinctly remembered the room at the end, mainly because the wall also served as a door. Katori slid the panel to the side and ushered us in. The other two remained at the door, turning their backs to us.

"What about them?" I asked.

"They are aware of what I am going to tell you. Please, remove your shoes and sit." She slid the panel back into place.

I took my boots off and set them aside, then sat in front of the small table that rested in the center of the room. I didn't bother using the pillows that were strewn around the sitting area. Maren took a seat beside me, and Katori sat on the other side of the table. The customary teapot and cups were absent.

"I expected Master Anesko to come himself, but given our history, I am not displeased to see you both."

"Why would Master Anesko come here?" Maren asked.

Katori frowned. "I sent word to him many weeks ago, asking for his help. I never received word back, so I assumed he would come in person. It seems I was mistaken."

"Master Anesko didn't send us," Maren said. "We came here of our own accord. What's going on? Where is everyone?"

"It is only Curates Domori and Haruna who remain, and myself. The others left after the dragons died."

"The dragons are dead?" Maren asked incredulously.

"Indeed," Katori replied. Her expression remained indifferent, but the sadness was visible in her eyes.

"We saw a skeleton down in the stable," I said. "How did the dragons die?"

"A wasting sickness took them. We used everything we had to treat them, but it was not enough in the end. The sickness spread quickly and soon there were no dragons left. I pleaded with the elder dragons in the mountain to come here, but they refused."

Maren shook her head sadly. "What was the sickness like?"

"It began slowly. Riders said that the bond would disappear. The dragons would fall into lethargic trances. Some of them never came out of it. As the days passed, it grew worse and spread until every dragon was affected. Within a few weeks, most of them had succumbed to the sickness. Those that didn't fled to the mountains."

"The dragon in the stable looked like it died a long time ago," I said. "A few weeks wouldn't cause that amount of deterioration, would it?"

"No," Katori confirmed. "That is another mystery. The sickness devoured the dragons, leaving nothing but their bones." She heaved a tired sigh. "I searched the stable for the source. I searched the forest. I searched, but I found nothing.

It seems that it came from nothing."

"Have you noticed anything else?" Maren asked.

"Yes. Magic is gone."

"What do you mean gone?"

"It does not exist anymore," Katori said. "The dragons died, and the magic left with them. Spells don't work. The *sutorīmu* has dried up."

"*Sutorīmu*?" I asked, stumbling over the word.

"The flow of magic," Maren explained.

I nodded.

"There is something else, but I do not know if it bears any importance. Before the sickness arrived, people came to the school with tales of ghosts. It was after you restored Demris, and I discounted them as old stories. Perhaps there is something more to those tales than I realized."

"Do you think these 'ghosts' had something to do with the sickness?" I asked.

"I do not believe so," Katori replied. "But that is only an assumption. My throat is parched. Would you like some tea?"

"Yes, please," Maren said.

I shook my head.

"I will return shortly."

Katori rose and left the room, sliding the panel shut behind her. Maren glanced at the panel, and the silhouettes of Domori and Haruna were visible. Maren pressed her finger to her lips and leaned close to me.

"Don't say anything to Katori about why we are here," she whispered.

"Why not? It sounds like what happened here is the same thing we're seeing in Osnen, only much worse."

"I know," Maren replied apprehensively. "She has enough on her plate. We shouldn't add to it."

I stared at her intently. There was more to it than that, but Maren seemed skittish to say anything else.

"What are we going to do?" I asked. "Katori looks half-starved, and there's no telling what those other two look like under their masks. They can't stay here."

"What do you suggest?"

"We should take them back to the Citadel."

"Sion and Demris can only carry two people, which means someone would be left behind. Not to mention the risk of one of them falling from the sky, or both of them. It's too risky."

"I'm open to ideas," I said.

Maren pursed her lips in thought. It was cute, and I leaned forward and pressed my lips to hers. Warmth spread throughout my body, followed by a tingly feeling. I pulled back, my heart racing in my chest. Every kiss we shared had that effect on me.

"Sir," Maren giggled. "What are you doing?"

The panel door slid open and Katori stepped inside. She carried a tray and set it down on the table as she sat, then lifted the teapot and filled the three cups that she'd brought. We all took a cup and sipped the hot tea in silence.

"If Master Anesko did not send you, why did you come here?"

I looked at Maren from my periphery. She swallowed her tea and wiped her lips with the back of her hand.

"We were passing through and decided to stop for a visit," she answered. "If we had any idea what was happening here, we'd have come long before now."

Katori stared at Maren. I wasn't sure if she believed Maren's false reason or not. Finally, Katori nodded.

"Where are you headed? I may be able to guide you on a quicker route."

I saw the hesitation etched on Maren's face. She didn't know what to say. I tried to think of something, but the only place nearby that came to mind was the Island of Lost Souls, and we certainly wouldn't be returning there.

"We're headed to the mountains," Maren said vaguely.

"To see the elder dragons?"

"Yes."

Katori's brow arched curiously. "What for?"

"For Eldwin."

Katori turned her gaze on me, and I tried not to squirm in discomfort.

"I, uh … have a wound that won't heal," I said. "We hoped they might have a cure."

Katori snorted. "The elder dragons are proud creatures. I wouldn't waste my time with them if I were you."

"I wouldn't if I didn't think they were the only ones who could help."

"Speaking of which, we should be going," Maren said. "The wound is infected, so we should see if they will help. We'll return here as soon as we're done," Maren added when Katori's expression turned downcast.

"Very well," Katori said. "I will await your return. It has been many days since we've seen someone who wasn't a vagabond."

Maren and I rose and put our boots back on, then Katori led us back out into the courtyard. She looked so sad to see us leaving that I had to turn away. Once we were in the field, I groaned.

"I feel terrible about leaving them," I said.

"I do, too," Maren replied. "But there's something I need to see first."

"What is it?"

"I think I know what's happening," she said. "And

it's all my fault."

7

"What are you talking about?"

Maren stopped walking, but she didn't look at me.

"What Katori said … about the ghosts. I know what they are."

"What are they?" I asked.

"Souls of the dead."

I stood there quietly, not sure what to say at first. "I don't understand. Souls of what dead? The dragons?"

"No, not just the dragons. All souls."

"How do you know?"

Maren turned to look at me. "I know it sounds insane, but we need to go where the ferryman was killed. I have to know for sure."

The ferryman. Demris's first victim from when he'd been brought back from the island. What did the ferryman have anything to do with … and then it hit me, and I understood Maren's logic.

"You think the ghosts are lost souls?"

"Yes."

"It seems plausible," I said. "But what do the souls have to do with what happened here at the school?"

"I'm not sure," Maren admitted. "Maybe nothing at all, but it's still something we need to look into. I hadn't considered it before, but if the ferryman is dead, how do the souls get to the island?"

"They walk on water?"

"No," Maren scoffed. "They can't touch water, which is why the ferryman took them on his boat."

I must have forgotten that detail. "All right. So we go and see if you are correct. And if you are? What then?"

"I haven't thought that far ahead yet."

I looked at Sion and Demris. They seemed to be doing well, but there was no telling how long that would last. Katori said that magic was gone. I feared how that would affect our dragons, considering their connection to it.

What do you think? I asked Sion. *Can you make it there?*

Yes.

And what about Demris?

There was a pause.

He says he can handle it.

"I'm on board," I said. "There's just one problem."

"What's that?"

"Last time we had a guide. Do you remember where this place is?"

I do, Sion said.

"Never mind. Sion knows the way. But we'll have to go on foot."

"Why? It'll be faster if we fly."

"We didn't fly last time. We walked there."

Maren frowned. "Why didn't we fly? I don't remember anything stopping us before."

Now that she mentioned it, I couldn't remember the reason either. There was a faint memory floating in the back of my mind, but when I tried to focus on it, the memory eluded me.

"I can't remember, either," I said.

"Then we fly." Maren smiled.

It would be faster. I shrugged, and we returned to Sion and Demris. Maren climbed into Demris's saddle and waited, both of them watching me. I rubbed Sion's snout and massaged along her neck, subconsciously trying to stall. I wasn't sure why, but I had a feeling that things were going to take a turn for the worse.

"We need to fly low," I said.

I climbed up Sion's shoulder and settled myself, then nodded at Maren. Demris launched into the sky, and Sion quickly followed after him, taking the lead. We kept low and headed south toward the Sea of Colisle, or The Wasted Deep as the locals called it. It wasn't far from the school, only a few miles, and the terrain slowly transformed from peaceful grassy plains to rough, uneven rocky ground.

Thinking back, I remembered our guide had mentioned that a volcanic eruption was responsible for the jagged landscape. It made me wonder if that eruption had been from the volcano on the Island of Lost Souls.

I didn't like that place, Sion said.

Neither did I. It was a living nightmare. How are you feeling?

I can feel something pulling at me, she replied. *It's like the magic of the flute, but much stronger.*

I patted Sion's shoulder. *Hang in there. As soon as we can confirm Maren's suspicions, we can get away from this cursed place.*

Demris is struggling. The pull is harder on him.

Why? I asked.

Because he's been to the other side of mortality.

Beside us, Demris began flying erratically. He swerved left and right, his wings flapping in an irregular pattern.

"Land!" I screamed. "Land!"

It seemed as if I was about to watch them fall from the sky again, but Demris managed to descend and came to a stop, using his claws to latch onto a rock that jutted up from the ground. Sion landed nearby, and I climbed down her shoulder and ran to Demris. He was heaving as though he'd been flying at break-neck speed, and foam had collected along the sides of his mouth. Maren leaped down from his back, worry creasing her face.

"The closer we get, the worse he becomes," she said. "I don't think he can make it there."

"There's a reason for that," I replied. "Whatever is pulling at them is hitting Demris much harder because he's been dead before."

Maren chewed on her lower lip. "How is that connected?" she asked.

I shrugged. "I don't know. I think we should go back."

"No!" Maren replied quickly. Her tone softened. "No," she repeated. "I need to know. We can leave Demris here to rest. Can Sion carry both of us?"

I think so, Sion answered.

"Yes, but we run the risk of the same thing happening to her." I let the words hang in the air. I didn't want any harm to come to either dragon and although something was affecting them even in Osnen, it certainly seemed worse here.

"I have to know," Maren said resolutely.

"Fine, but we aren't flying. Sion can take us there on foot."

Maren looked like she was going to argue, but she nodded instead. She gently touched the side of Demris's face and whispered to him. He growled in reply, but it was pitiful and didn't seem to be an objection.

She turned away from him and climbed onto Sion's back, leaving room in front of her for me. I stared at Demris for a moment, concerned about him. He didn't look so good. The green of his scales, already dull, seemed to be fading even more.

"Let's hurry," I said.

I joined Maren in the saddle and Sion began running south. The terrain was worse here, the rocks that littered the area sharp and jagged. Sion's claws scratched along them, the scraping sounds loud and jarring. We were almost within sight of the beach when Sion slowed her pace.

I can't breathe, she complained. *Get off my back.*

"We walk on our own from here," I said, standing. I offered Maren my hand, helping her up, then we slipped down to the ground.

Do you need to stay here? I asked Sion.

No, I just can't carry you anymore. It's difficult enough fighting off the pull of my energy.

"Is she all right?" Maren asked, glancing at Sion uncertainly.

"She will be," I replied. "Come on, we're almost there."

We continued on foot, carefully navigating along the serrated rocks. I would never have imagined we'd come back to this place, not after everything we'd experienced. A faint tune reached my ears, and I involuntarily flinched. It resembled the music of the dragon bone flutes, but it wasn't painful. It was a keening sound, filled with sorrow, and it was vaguely familiar.

"Do you hear that?" Maren asked lowly.

"Yes."

As we closed the distance to the beach, the rocks gave way to low rolling hills of sand. The sound of crashing waves overshadowed the sad tune, and I found myself walking faster. Maren kept pace with me, and Sion was a few feet behind us.

How are you feeling? I asked.

It's getting harder to focus. Whatever is ahead of us is the source.

The source of the pull on you?

Yes.

That wasn't a good thing. Maren was magicless, and Sion was probably on the verge of succumbing to unconsciousness. I looked at Maren from my periphery. Her expression was focused, her gaze locked straight ahead.

You can stay behind if you need to, I said.

No, Sion replied. *I am coming with you.*

I debated telling her she had to stay behind, but I knew that would be futile. She was as stubborn as Maren, if not more so. Sion snickered through the bond and I couldn't help but smile.

We began ascending a large sandhill. My legs burned as the sand pulled at my boots, making the climb arduous. The sound of the waves grew louder, and I imagined I could feel the splashing mist of the water as the waves crashed upon the shore. Overhead, a few seagulls cried out and fled as they spotted Sion.

I reached the top of the rise first. Waves rolled along the surface of the sea, washing onto the shore before slipping away again. I continued down the other side and stopped at a steep drop that led down to the beach. My breath caught in my throat when I spotted an overturned boat. It was the ferryman's. Or rather, it had been before he died.

Maren caught up, stopping beside me. Sion issued a gleeful roar and jumped, gliding down to the beach and stepping in the water. She sniffed the boat, then turned and looked at me.

Do you see them? She asked.

See who?

As if on command, ghostly figures began flickering in and out of sight.

8

There were hundreds of them, maybe thousands.

"Gods," I breathed. "There are so many."

Maren waved her hand toward the souls. "This is all my fault."

"No, it's not."

"Yes, it is. Demris killed the ferryman, Eldwin. If I wouldn't have brought Demris back from the island, he'd still be alive."

I couldn't argue with that, but how could she have known what would happen? How could anyone? Maren made her way down to the beach, and I followed after her. The souls glowed with a green aura, and memories of being on the island came flooding back to me.

Sion growled suddenly. The souls were approaching her, encircling her massive form. She had nowhere to go but up, and she leaped into the air. Her wings flapped a few times, but she couldn't gain momentum and landed back on the beach.

They're trying to kill me! Sion screamed.

I sprinted ahead, drawing my sword and swinging at the souls. It did nothing to them. The blade passed through their incorporeal shapes, disrupting their presence for only a moment before they flickered back into existence.

"Stop!" I demanded. "Leave my dragon alone!"

The disembodied face of an elf appeared in front of me, the rest of his body appearing moments later.

"Help," his voice rasped.

"Help," another chimed in, a dwarf.

A chorus of voices begging for aid erupted around me. Their focus had been removed from Sion, thankfully, but it was impossible to know how long that would last.

"We need to help them," Maren said, walking through the crowd of souls.

"How exactly do you propose we do that?"

"With that." She pointed at the boat.

"No," I said, shaking my head. "There's no way I'm getting on that thing ever again."

"Then stay here, but I'm going. At least help me flip it over."

I hesitantly left Sion and walked over to the boat, sheathing my sword. The souls followed us, crowding around the overturned vessel. The wood was old and deteriorated, but it was still mostly intact. The back end of the boat had pieces of wood missing, and I doubted it would get far before sinking.

"You can't get in this," I said. "Look at it. It's falling apart."

"The souls need to get to the island," Maren replied. "This is the only way."

The ghostly visages wavered in and out of existence, their cries for help tearing at my heart. Death should be the end of suffering, and yet, these souls were still struggling to find peace. I grabbed onto the boat and waited for Maren to take the other side, then we heaved together. Despite the boat's dilapidated appearance, it was heavy. I grunted from the exertion and had to give up for a moment.

"How is this blasted thing so heavy? It's barely even holding together!"

"Calm down," Maren said. "We've got this."

I took a deep breath and set my feet in place, then prepared to lift the boat again.

"One. Two. Three," Maren counted off.

We heaved again, and I put all of my strength into the effort. The boat slowly tilted upward, and after a moment of agonizing struggle, it rolled over. I groaned with relief, and couldn't help but laugh. My arm muscles burned fiercely.

"Now we need to push it into the water," Maren said.

"You're going to have to give me a minute," I replied. "My arms are useless right now."

I looked around at the crowd of souls that surrounded us and considered how small the boat was.

"How long do you plan on doing this?" I asked.

"What do you mean?"

"All of them aren't going to fit in one trip."

Realization dawned on her face, but she shrugged. "However long it takes, I guess."

I could tell by her tone that she'd already made her decision. I sighed. There would be no dissuading her now. Once my arms stopped burning, I joined her at the back of the boat and we pushed it through the wet sand to the water.

"Hold it still," Maren said.

I did as she asked and kept the boat steady so she could climb into it. She bent over and fumbled around before standing back up with the paddles. They'd been tucked into a long pocket space, and I wondered who had put them there.

"I'm coming with you," I said, though I dreaded it.

"I know," Maren replied with a smile. "You wouldn't leave me alone out here. You love me too much."

"That, and Demris would personally chew my head from my body."

Maren laughed. "Probably."

"Wait here. I need to get Sion."

I hurried across the beach to Sion and retrieved the magical collar from her saddle, as well as a plain robe, and prayed that its magic wasn't affected.

If the souls are trying to steal your life energy, you don't need to stay here with them.

Put the collar on, Sion said.

I slipped it around her neck and waited. A moment later, Sion's body began shrinking in size. Her red scales flattened and paled, slowly transforming into human flesh. The magic still worked. Sion stood before me, a red-haired naked woman. I handed her the robe and she covered herself, then we joined Maren in the boat.

A small host of souls swarmed onto the vessel. Another group tried to join us, but an unseen force stopped them. They wailed in despair.

"I'll come back for you," Maren said. "All of you!"

That seemed to placate them, and they began milling around the beach. Maren sat down and began paddling, guiding us out from the shore and into the misty fog that hovered over the water. Even though it was midday, the light failed to pierce the shroud. As we floated into it, everything around us dimmed.

I remembered our trip across the sea before and kept away from the edges of the boat. The haunting tune from earlier drifted on the air, but this time, voices mingled with it, begging me to get into the water.

Ignore them, Sion said. *They have no power over you.*

As the temptation to jump into the sea intensified, I wasn't so sure about that. Maren rowed in silence until she started talking to herself. I looked at her questioningly.

"Did you say something?"

"I'm talking to one of the souls," she said. "Don't you see him?"

I shook my head.

"He's standing near me. He wants to know why he's had to wait so long to get to the island."

"Did you tell him it's complicated?"

"Pretty much," Maren replied.

"Your magic is working now, I take it?"

"No. I still can't feel it. There isn't even a trickle of it."

I frowned. If she didn't have access to her magic, how could she see the souls if they weren't flickering into existence?

Do you see them? I asked Sion.

Yes.

Why can't I?

I don't know. I see them as I see you and Maren, but they glow a little. That's how I know the difference.

Maren continued speaking with the soul. I stared intently where she was looking, trying to force my eyes into seeing the specter. After a long while, I gave up. Sion's mirth at my failed attempt filled the bond.

Will I ever be able to cast magic through our bond? I asked.

Only time will tell. I do not control such things.

Maren looked at me, her expression one of concern.

"What is it?" I instinctively gripped the hilt of my sword.

"I know what the source is," she said. "The problem with magic."

I waited expectantly.

"It's the souls."

"How?"

"Lost souls must go to the island until their time is due," Maren replied. "Since they cannot cross over water, the ferryman is supposed to take them. And since said ferryman is dead, they've been stuck on the beach."

"What does that have to do with magic?"

"I'm getting to that. The souls have been siphoning it to stay alive."

I furrowed my brow. "To stay alive? But they're dead."

"Sorry, I'm not explaining it correctly. Apparently, the souls are renewed by the magic of the island, and if they don't arrive there, they'll fade from existence. In order to keep that from happening, they've been feeding off our flow of magic."

That made sense. It was also concerning.

"What about our dragons? Is their illness

connected to that?"

"Yes. Dragons are the most sensitive creatures to magic that we know of, and that's why they are getting sick. As the souls continue to drain the flow of magic, the dragons are feeling it in their very being."

"That would explain why the dragons at Katori's school died so quickly," I said. "They're closer to where the souls are gathered."

Maren nodded. "Exactly."

"So if we ferry the souls across to the island, that will fix everything?"

"I can't say for certain, but I think it should. There a problem with that, though."

"What?"

"People die every day," Maren said. "The task will never be complete."

"Then we need to find a new ferryman, someone who will devote their life to the task like the last one."

"Do you know of anyone?" Maren asked, laughing.

"That will be a challenge," I admitted. "We will do what we can for now and take this information back to Anesko. The Order can figure out what to do from there."

"We can hope," Maren replied.

The fog eventually faded and the island came

into view. Maren guided the boat ahead, grounding it on the shore. As the souls departed and stepped onto the island, they became visible to me. I watched them leave, marching their way deeper into the island. The last soul to appear turned to Maren and offered a bow.

"Thank you, ferryman," he said, then walked off to join the others.

9

"Helping them feels good," Maren said as we headed back to the mainland.

She paddled at a quick pace, and the boat glided along the water effortlessly as if it wasn't on the verge of falling apart.

"I'm sure they appreciate it," I replied. "Languishing on the beach for months while slowly fading from existence isn't something anyone would enjoy, dead or not. And, hopefully, the flow of magic will return to normal once there aren't as many souls feeding off of it."

"Yes, I hope that is the case." Maren sighed wistfully. "I don't feel like myself without magic."

We reached the shore, and another group of souls climbed aboard. Just as before, a barrier kept the others at bay. We pushed off the beach and turned the boat around, then headed back for the island. It seemed like such a lonely existence to travel back and forth with only the dead for company. The ferryman had seemed content with his lot in life, so maybe I was wrong, but it certainly wasn't for me.

And so it went, back and forth. We picked up a group, drifted through the fog, dropped them off, and returned to do it all over again. Maren spoke with the souls as she rowed, asking questions about their lives. Sion watched and listened, but for me, it was a one-sided conversation. Sion offered to fill in the blanks, but it wasn't the same.

Eventually, I contented myself by staring off the side of the boat, looking for the source of the haunting song. It was a fruitless effort, though, as the fog blanketed everything. I could see roughly a foot of water beside the boat, but past that, it was like staring into the clouds. My reverie was broken as we reached the island, and I'd lost count of how many times we'd made the journey. The souls departed, and we began the trip back once more.

"Once we hit land again, I'm going to take a break," Maren said. "My arms are killing me."

"Do you want me to take over for a while?"

"No, I'm fine for now."

I nodded and looked over the side again as we entered the fog. The song drifted on the air, stronger this time. It sounded closer, too. The words were faint, barely recognizable by ear, but they echoed within my mind.

Come and see,

What lies beneath,

The foggy and misty,

Surface of the sea.

The words tugged at me, and the desire to see what mystery was hidden under the water became so strong, I stood up. Maren was rowing and looking ahead, and Sion was dozing off at the rear of the boat. I would be in and out before they knew

I was gone. I stepped over the side and dropped into the water.

I expected the water to be cold, but it was surprisingly warm. I treaded in place, looking around for the music, but the sound seemed to come from everywhere at once. The chorus changed, and the only words echoing now were *come and see, come and see.*

"What lies beneath," I whispered.

Inhaling a deep breath, I plunged under the water's surface. It was murky, but here and there, thin shafts of sunlight penetrated the darkness. Something moved in my periphery, but when I turned to look, there was nothing.

You're almost there, multiple voices said at the same time.

I peered left and right, but still, there was nothing but dark water. How had the voices spoken underwater? I spotted movement again and turned to look, and this time something was there. Or rather, someone.

It was a woman.

Long, golden blond hair rippled in the water around her, framing a beautiful face. Her eyes were icy blue, and she smiled as she beckoned me to swim closer. I was drawn inexplicably to her beauty and kicked my feet, cutting through the water until she was within arm's length. And then I noticed two more women.

They all resembled one another, and I assumed

they were siblings. One of them seemed shy, and she continuously glanced at me in a playful manner. I wanted to say something, to ask them who they were and how they ended up down here, but I was holding my breath. My lungs started to burn, but I ignored the pain and stared at the women.

It must have been the distraction of their beauty, but I became aware that they weren't wearing anything over their chests. My eyes went down further, but the rest of their bodies were lost in the murkiness. Soft hands touched my shoulders, and I looked back to see two more women. They smiled, but something wasn't right. A voice was shouting a warning in the back of my mind.

Come with us, one of them said.

Yes, come with us, the others repeated.

Eldwin!

It was the voice warning me again.

Eldwin, stay away from them!

Why? They seem friendly.

The voice growled in my mind, and the reaction seemed familiar somehow. Something splashed into the water beside me, something big. An enormous head snaked past me, its jaws snapping at the women. I recoiled in terror as the beauty of the women faded, their skin shriveling before my eyes, revealing their true hideous appearances.

I felt as if I was waking from a dream. My thoughts were fuzzy, and I realized I was underwater. Panic gripped me as my lungs constricted.

Where am I? I screamed within my mind.

The giant head, which I now realized was Sion, snapped at another of the creatures, sending them fleeing into the darkness below.

Grab onto me! Sion demanded.

I swam to her and tightly gripped the saddle horn with my hands. Sion sped forward, then angled down. My lungs felt like they were going to burst, and I clenched my jaw, biting my lips to keep them from opening. My vision erupted with stars. I needed air. Sion changed direction and swam upward. A shaft of light stabbed through the water, illuminating something below. I only glimpsed it before the light disappeared, but it looked like a building.

Sion broke the surface of the water just as my body forced my mouth open. I gasped, still clutching the saddle. The boat was a few feet away, and Maren was standing in it. I wasn't sure, but it looked like tears were streaming down her cheeks.

How are you in dragon form? I asked.

Maren removed the collar so I could rescue you.

I'm sorry.

Sion didn't reply, but she wasn't angry with me. The bond was filled with a mix of concern and relief.

We'll meet Maren on the shore.

Before I could protest, Sion flapped her wings, lifting us out of the water. She gained altitude, then flew ahead of the small boat. Droplets of water ran along Sion's scales, pushed by the wind. As clarity filled my mind, I realized what had happened. The sirens had tricked me.

I should have been more alert, Sion said. It sounded like she was berating herself.

It was my fault for not fighting off their song, I replied.

We reached the shore within a few minutes, and Sion landed gently on the beach. The souls were still there, wandering aimlessly though their wailing had ceased. I slipped down the side of her body and ran my hands vigorously through my hair, flinging the water free. Sion was watching me, her gaze roaming up and down.

What is it?

Did they bite you? She asked.

No, why?

Good.

Why? I repeated.

Their bite is poisonous. It can kill within hours.

Thank you for saving me.

Sion nuzzled me, driving her snout into my stomach. I tumbled backward, using my arms to break my fall. The wound on my left arm flared with pain. I'd almost forgotten it was there as it hadn't bothered me for a while now. I glanced down and realized the bandage was gone. It must have come off in the water.

The skin was red and swollen, and the slash where the goblin's rusty blade had struck me was grotesque. It looked infected. I got up and walked into the water to wash the sand from my clothes, then stomped back up the beach. I waited and watched the water until the boat came into view. Maren was rowing slowly, her face red from the exertion. The boat hit the shore and Maren climbed out.

"Eldwin! Are you all right?"

She ran toward me, but after she got a few feet from the boat, she abruptly stopped, a look of confusion on her face. She took a step back and stretched out her arms as if feeling for something, then tried to go forward again.

"What are you doing?" I asked, walking to where she was.

"I can't move past here," she said. "Something is stopping me."

"What do you mean?" I stepped past her, then turned around and walked back. Nothing hindered me.

Maren tried again, but she couldn't get any further. I grabbed onto her hands and pulled, but she was held firmly in place.

"I don't understand," she said.

"I don't either. I'm able to move through

whatever this is." I motioned toward the air in front of her.

A group of souls had gathered around us, and one of them moved close to Maren. His ghostly face was twisted in a pained expression, but his words were clear.

"You can't leave the boat," it said.

"Why not?" Maren asked.

"The ferryman is bound to the vessel."

"The ferryman is dead," she replied.

The face smiled, but there was no joy in its eyes.

"You *are* the ferryman."

10

"What did you say?" I asked.

The soul turned to me, the smile on his warped visage an eerie addition.

"She is the ferryman," he said. "She stepped onto the vessel and held the paddles. The enchantment has been made."

"What enchantment?" I looked from the soul to Maren. "Do you know what he's talking about?"

"In theory, yes," Maren replied. "I know how magic works, so I understand what he's saying, but I don't understand why. Why me? Why now?"

"There must be a way to break the enchantment," I said.

"Possibly, but old magic is hard to destroy. Without access to magic, there's nothing I can do to try and break it."

I looked at Sion.

I'm not a sorcerer, she said.

Is there anything you can try?

Not against that kind of magic. It's more powerful than I am.

"I'm hungry," Maren said. Her words kept me from descending into helplessness.

"I've got a little bit of food left."

I retrieved my remaining rations from Sion's saddle. The leather bag that held them was wet, but it had kept the food mostly dry. I had half a loaf of bread, some cheese, and a few grapes that hadn't been crushed. Although the sun was shining, I felt cold. My body shivered, and Maren watched me with a worried expression.

"It's your wound," she said.

"Among other things, I'm sure."

"It's infected, Eldwin. Did you not go to the infirmary as Anesko asked?"

"I didn't have time," I replied. "Besides, we have bigger things to worry about right now."

"We should make a fire. Your lips are turning blue."

"Good idea," I said.

Driftwood littered the beach, providing the perfect source for a fire. Some of the pieces were soaked, but that didn't stop Sion's flames from igniting them. Within a few minutes, we had a small fire burning and we sat around it as we ate. The heat helped to dry my clothes. I pulled my boots off and pointed my feet near the flames.

"What happened out there?" Maren asked. "With the sirens, I mean."

"Their song overpowered me. Before I realized what was happening, I was in the water looking for them."

"Did you see them?"

A shiver ran down my back and I nodded. "Yes, I saw them. They appeared beautiful at first, but once Sion was in the water, their beauty faded and I saw them for what they truly are. Monsters."

"Sion noticed you were gone before I did," Maren said lowly. "I feared I lost you."

"As long as I have breath in my lungs, you'll never lose me," I replied.

Maren grabbed onto my mangled hand and squeezed it. We remained quiet for a long while. I watched the flames of the fire dance about and wondered how we would get out of this predicament.

"Why a boat?" I asked.

"What do you mean?"

"Why a boat? Why not a bridge or something bigger? People don't live forever, so why create a means of transporting souls that requires a mortal person that will eventually die? A bridge would have been smarter."

"Who could build a bridge that far?" Maren asked.

I shrugged. "Sorcerers?"

"Even magic has its limits."

"I know, but a bridge would allow souls access at all times instead of having to wait on a boat. If there was a bridge, we wouldn't have the mess we do now."

"It might be possible, but it would require a lot

of magic to create something like that, which is probably why whoever made this used a boat. It's much easier to enchant a smaller item. Besides, considering how little magic there is right now, it would be an impossible task."

I scratched my chin, the gears in my mind spinning wildly. "What about the bone flute?"

"What about it?" Maren asked.

"It's supposed to channel magic, right? So could you use it to generate enough magic to create a bridge?"

Maren was oddly silent. "I don't know."

I had an idea, but it would require leaving Maren behind. At least, for a short period of time. "I can go get it," I said.

"No, you can't."

"Why not?"

"I destroyed it," Maren replied.

My hopes crashed like the waves on the beach. "Why did you destroy it?"

"It was an instrument built for evil purposes. I couldn't stand to let it fall into the wrong hands."

She was right, but that still ruined my only idea. "Is there anything else that could produce that much magic?"

"Enchanted items could be used," Maren said. "They are imbued with magic, and if you unweave the spells, it frees up that magical energy to be used for something else.”

“So if I found enough magical items, we could create a bridge?”

“It would take a lot of items.”

“Or a few very powerful ones,” I said. “Right?”

Maren nodded. “Yes, but where would you get them? Items that powerful aren’t just lying around somewhere.”

“We have two already,” I said.

“What are you babbling about? We don’t have a single one,” Maren replied.

“Sure we do. The boat is one, and Sion’s collar is the other.”

Maren laughed. “That’s genius, but we still have a problem. Even if you manage to find some more items we can use, there’s no magic to unweave the spells with. Magic requires magic.”

“That’s the only flaw in my plan,” I said. “Maybe as you ferry the souls across, you’ll remove enough that magic starts flowing again.”

Maren stared out at the sea. The souls were crowding around the boat, waiting for their opportunity to rush into it. I supposed they weren’t able to get in if the ferryman wasn’t onboard. Magic was amazing. And odd.

I noticed one of the souls sitting by the fire. He stared out at the sea the same as Maren. There was something familiar about him. His head turned completely around to look at me, but his body stayed put.

"The helmsman!" I shouted, pointing.

The soul looked the same as he had in life. He was thin and frail-looking, with a scraggly beard that hung from his chin. His eyebrows were thick and bushy, with rogue hairs pointing in every direction. His head, however, was completely devoid of any hair.

"Look who finally decided to come back," he said, his voice just as raspy as I remembered.

"We've been busy," I replied, though it sounded like a lame excuse.

The helmsman harrumphed and rolled his eyes. "I've been listening to your conversation, and you have the beginnings of a good idea. A bridge would be a much better way for the dead to cross over to the island, but as your friend mentioned, magic is in a bit of a quandary right now."

"Do you have any suggestions?" I asked. "About how to lessen the siphoning on magic?"

The helmsman cleared his throat and spit into the fire, but nothing happened. He clearly didn't realize that he didn't have to do such things since he was dead.

"I can't say how you can get enough magic to unweave the spells, because I don't know the answer to that, but I can tell you where you can find some powerful stuff."

"Where?" Maren asked, leaning forward.

"At the dragon rider school," he answered.

"Master Katori's school?"

"The same."

"Does she know these things are there?" I asked. "Or will this be news to her?"

"I couldn't say for certain, but I suspect she knows a little about them. The school is built upon an ancient temple, and that temple holds something dark and sinister inside. She would be a fool if she didn't at least know about the temple."

Maren and I exchanged looks.

"I don't want to leave you," I said, though I knew I would have to.

"I know, but we must make sacrifices. I will hold onto the hope that you won't be gone long."

"When you're ferrying souls, the time passes more quickly than you'd imagine," the helmsman said.

I pulled Maren close and pressed my lips to hers. She wrapped her arms around me, hugging me tightly. I never wanted to leave her embrace, but life wasn't about such things, only dreams were. We broke apart and I put my boots back on, then stood up.

"Please make sure Demris is all right," Maren said. "I feel his presence in the bond, but he feels far away."

"I will," I promised. I looked at the helmsman. "Take care of her for me, will you?"

"What can I do?" he replied. "I'm dead."

I didn't know what to say to that, so I shrugged. "I'll be back as quickly as I can."

"You know where to find me," Maren replied, smiling sadly.

It tore at my heart to leave her. I nodded and turned away so that she couldn't see my eyes watering. Sion stretched her wings and lowered herself to the ground so I could climb up her shoulder. I blinked rapidly to clear my eyes, then looked at Maren one more time before Sion launched into the air.

We flew north, following the same route we'd taken to get to the beach. My mind was swirling with thoughts and emotions, and I felt Sion close her end of the bond. I was probably overwhelming her senses, but I couldn't help it. The sandy hills faded, replaced by the jagged terrain of black volcanic rocks.

I spotted the area where we'd left Demris, and Sion flew low as we neared it. It would be hard to miss his giant green body, but I didn't see him anywhere. There were no signs of trouble, but there was no mistaking it.

Demris was gone.

11

Where could he have gone?

Perhaps he returned to the school, Sion said. *I can sense him, but I can't communicate with him. He might still be weak.*

Let's continue to the school, then. I desperately hoped that's where Demris was.

We turned northwest and flew over the rough terrain until I saw the tall grass that grew outside of the school. It was still so odd to see the place deserted. Sion landed outside the walls, and I dismounted and entered through the gates. I didn't see Demris anywhere, which worried me.

"Katori!" I shouted, her name echoing off the buildings around me.

I tried entering the main edifice, but it was barred again. Attempting the trick that Katori had done with the frame didn't work, and so I knocked on the door and waited. No one came. I walked around to the back where the stable was and stood at the entrance, staring down into the darkness.

"Katori! Are you down there?"

I heard footsteps approaching behind me and turned to look. It wasn't Katori. Two men wielding swords eyed me warily. They were disheveled and their clothes were dirty. The two couldn't have been more different in appearance. One was tall and slim, with short gray hair and a thin, unkempt beard. The other was stout and muscular. His hair was black and he was cleanly shaven.

"Toss over your sword," the gray-haired man said. "And then your coins."

I rested my hand on the hilt of my blade, trying to keep a non-threatening stance.

"I'm sorry, but that's not going to happen."

The shorter man looked at his friend for guidance. They must not have met much resistance in their thievery.

"Who are you, anyway? Why are you on the school grounds?" I asked.

"Are you a rider?" It was the gray-haired man again.

"I am."

"You aren't from this school," he said.

"No, I'm from Osnen."

"Did you know that Master Katori killed our dragons? Is that why you have come—to execute justice against her?"

They thought Katori killed their dragons? That was odd. I shook my head slowly.

"She did not kill the dragons. It was something else that caused their deaths."

"The wasting sickness," the man spat angrily. "I've heard the excuse many times. Katori is a liar. She will say anything to save her own skin."

"I can't change your mind if you've already decided on the matter," I replied. "Either way, you aren't getting my sword or my gold. I suggest you leave the grounds before my dragon gets wind of you."

Do you need me? Sion asked.

I think I've got it handled, I said.

"The red one is yours, then. What of the green one?"

So Demris *was* here.

"He belongs to my friend."

The man offered a slight nod. "We can sell him even if he's bonded."

"He's not for sale."

"Then we are at an impasse," the man said. "We aren't leaving without something. Either your coin or the dragon, though we would prefer the dragon."

Cut them down, Sion growled.

While I didn't agree with her, I was getting tired of their idle threats. I drew my sword and stabbed the tip into the ground.

"Please leave," I said. "I don't want trouble."

"Another fool," the gray-haired man said. "A pity."

The short man rushed me, swinging his sword in an 'X' pattern. I brought my blade up and side-stepped, kicking the man's right leg as he passed me. He tripped and tumbled to the ground, his sword clanging as it fell beside him.

The older man stalked toward me with measured steps. He wasn't as eager as his counterpart, which meant he likely had more training. We circled each other, our eyes locked. I didn't want to fight him. Regardless of whether I could best him, I didn't see the point. He thought Katori was a killer of dragons. Perhaps his mind was lost to madness over the loss of his dragon. I couldn't fault him for that. I'd experienced the feeling, however brief, and it had almost crippled me.

"You can still leave," I said, nodding toward the gates.

"I'd rather kill you first. That way, I get your gold *and* the dragons."

A wave of anger washed over me and I charged him. He brought his sword up defensively, his left arm angling behind his blade. His movements were graceful and fluid, his style foreign and exotic. I slashed my sword at him, but he swung his blade down, smacking mine aside. His left arm jabbed forward, his fingertips knifing me in the throat.

I coughed and staggered back, but he didn't take advantage of my momentary weakness. Instead, he waited until I recovered before attacking again. The man had some sense of honor, though it conflicted with his attempt to rob me.

He spun around, his blade held out wide, extending his reach. I misjudged the distance and grunted as the flat side of his sword struck my left shoulder. The strike stung my flesh, the force also jarring my wound.

"Do you surrender?"

"Of course not," I snapped.

"You are too slow," the man said. "And you are outnumbered."

The shorter man was back on his feet, his face red with anger. He came at me from one side while the older man attacked from the other. I ducked and spun, but their blades continuously hit their mark. It quickly became evident that they were toying with me.

If they were vagabonds, I could have easily been able to overtake them. But these men weren't common thieves, they were trained riders. That made them evenly matched with me, but their fighting style was so different from my own that I was having trouble defending myself. I was breathing heavily and growing tired, but they barely seemed affected.

The stout man got close enough to land a kick to the back of my leg, knocking me down. The gray-haired man pressed his blade to my neck, the tip jabbing painfully against my flesh.

"This has been fun, but now the game is over. Your life is mine."

Sion roared from the field and I knew she was on her way, but she would be too late. Still, the knowledge that she would rip them limb from limb after I was dead consoled me. Not much, though.

"Cease this immediately!"

Leaning my head up slightly, I spotted Katori striding across the courtyard, followed by Domori and Haruna. The stout man charged them with a war cry. Domori stepped around Katori and engaged the man. Their battle was brief, and then Domori struck a killing blow. The stout man collapsed, a choking sound escaping his lips. The gray-haired man removed his blade from my neck and turned to face Katori.

"You were banished from this place," Katori said. "Why are you here?"

"He's trying to steal Maren's dragon," I replied.

Katori scowled at the man. "First you dishonor the school, then you dishonor yourself?"

"I have more honor than you, dragon slayer."

"I am no dragon slayer," Katori said. "If you removed the blindfold from your eyes, you would see the truth of the matter."

"I've never seen more clearly than I do now. My new master has removed the falsehoods you brainwashed me with."

"Do not dare speak his name," Katori snarled. "He walks the path of darkness and was cast out long ago."

"You may have exiled Kage, but he is rising anew like the phoenix. His cleansing flames will wash over Terran with fury, then the rest of the world will know his name."

I had no idea who or what they were talking about. I rolled away from the man and scrambled to my feet, but he didn't even glance at me. He kept his gaze locked on Katori.

"Kage will have his head removed from his body if I ever see him again."

"Those are strong words for someone without a dragon. Or magic."

"I wouldn't be so sure of that," Katori said.

The man snorted, but Katori lifted her hand and a ball of flame erupted from her palm, shooting up a few feet into the air before fading. The gray-haired man's bluster faded a bit.

"Leave or die," Katori offered.

The man looked at me, then back at Katori. He had to know he would be fighting a losing battle. After a tense moment, he sheathed his blade and walked away without another word, exiting the grounds through the gate.

Don't kill him, I told Sion as she swooped into the courtyard.

I will do as I please, she growled.

Demris is in the stable. Will you check on him?

Sion rumbled to herself, but she stalked over to the stable entrance and disappeared belowground.

"Your magic has returned?" I asked, looking at Katori.

She offered a sly smile. "No. That was merely

sleight of hand and flash powder. When Demris returned by himself, I feared the worst," she said. "I am glad to see you and your dragon are well, but where is Maren?"

"It's a long story," I said.

"I have time."

"Who was that?" I asked. "And what was he talking about?"

"That was Akada. He was one of the riders who left after the dragons died." Katori shook her head, a sad expression on her face. "He sought out Kage, a fallen rider who claimed I was responsible for the sickness that killed the dragons. He breathes many threats, but he dares not attack me openly."

"What is a fallen rider?"

"Let us go inside and I will explain," Katori said.

We walked to the main building and Katori opened the door the same way she had previously. I was certain I did the motion on the frame the same as she did, but it hadn't worked for me. Once inside, Domori and Haruna left us alone.

"Kage sought power that was not his to have," Katori said, guiding me along the hall. "He was cast out by Master Tsunejiro before his death. After I assumed the role of master, Kage began convincing other riders to join his cause."

"He sounds like a real thorn," I said.

"Yes, he is. Tell me, where is Maren?"

I took a deep breath and told her everything.

12

Katori sipped tea from a wooden cup as she stared off. Her left eye twitched, and she blinked, breaking from her reverie. She turned her gaze on me. The haunted look in her eyes that I'd seen before was gone, but she still didn't appear to be herself.

"The helmsman is correct," she said. "There is an ancient temple under the school."

"And it has magic items we could use?"

"That I do not know. I have never been down there before. My master forbade it upon pain of death."

"It sounds like there is something down there, then."

"Yes, there is *something* down there," Katori said. "My people call it the enenra."

"What's that?"

"It is a powerful creature, one that has never been defeated."

"How do you know it's still alive? I imagine there's not much food in an abandoned temple," I said.

Katori shook her head. "You do not understand. The enenra is not a living creature, it is …" she struggled to find the right words. "Like a soul, but different."

"Different how?"

"So many questions," Katori muttered, but she was smiling. "The legends say that enenra are created when someone dies being burned. They are rare, but very dangerous and almost impossible to kill because they are made of smoke."

I tried to imagine such a creature and shuddered.

"The legends also say that the enenra can merge with a living person, taking over their body. I believe that is why my master did not want anyone going into the temple."

"If that thing really is down there, that's going to pose a problem. We need the items that the helmsman claims are in that temple." Katori glowered at me. "If you'll let me go in there," I added.

"Do I have a choice?" she asked.

"Not unless we're going to leave Maren bound to that boat. And if you don't want magic back for a while. I saw how few souls she can ferry at one time. It'll probably take months before the flow of magic is back to normal."

Katori frowned, but I knew she was seriously considering it.

"The worst thing that could happen is that we find the enenra. We'll just hightail it out of there."

"The temple doors are warded," Katori said. "There's an amulet that will dispel it, but I don't know how we'd restore the wards without magic. It is a great risk."

"Then we'll kill it."

"How do you kill something made of smoke?" she asked.

"I … don't know," I admitted. "Do your legends mention anything about that?"

"Not that I can remember. I don't think it is a good idea to enter that place. My master did not fear it without reason."

"I can't save Maren without you," I said, choking back my emotions. "I need your help."

Katori stared into her wooden cup and went quiet. I didn't want to make an enemy of her, but if she refused to help me, then I would find the amulet and go down there alone. Well, not quite alone. I'd have Sion with me. A shadow crossed over Katori's face. She drank the rest of her tea and set the cup down.

"I will help you," she said. "Domori and Haruna will come with us as well. Will you bring your dragon?"

"Yes, Sion will come with us. I still have the magical collar."

"The tunnel that leads to the temple is large enough to accommodate her, but it would be wise to bring it."

That made me feel a little less anxious about encountering a creature made of smoke. With Sion there as a dragon instead of a human, she'd pose more of a threat. At least, that's what I hoped.

"Thank you, Katori. This means a lot to me."

"I offer my help because you are my friend, but there is something else. Once we find a way to free Maren of the enchantment, you must help me with a task."

"What is it?" I asked.

"It is not for you to know yet. You must trust me."

I did trust Katori, but her request seemed odd. If it solidified her help, though, I wouldn't decline her. I nodded slowly. "I will help you," I said. "After Maren is free."

"Good. I will need to prepare with Domori and Haruna. You may rest here until we are ready."

Katori left me in the small room with food and plenty of tea to drink. I ate my fill and ended up falling asleep on the floor. A while later, Katori returned with the two Curates and we left the building.

We're on our way, I told Sion. *How's Demris?*

He's conscious, but he's still weak.

Does he know about Maren?

Yes. He's not happy.

Neither am I, but we're working on finding a solution. Did you tell him that?

Yes. He says if you fail, he'll eat you.

I laughed. *You wouldn't let that happen, would you?*

I don't know. Demris is stronger than me.

We both laughed through the bond. When we reached the stable, Domori and Haruna retrieved torches and set them ablaze. Domori took the lead, followed by Katori and myself, and Haruna took the rear of the line.

The tunnel we followed took us to where Sion and Demris were. Sion joined our group, walking behind Haruna, and Demris remained in his cave. He glared at me as we left, and I wondered if he truly would try to eat me. I reminded myself that failure wasn't an option, and therefore Demris would have no reason to try.

We marched on and on, and it seemed to me that there would be no end. My imagination ran rampant, and I wondered if we had crossed into some sort of portal that went on forever. Perhaps the enenra knew we were coming, and he'd spirited us away somewhere. It also didn't help that I felt like we were being followed. The ground gradually descended until we reached a dead end.

"Did we go the wrong way?" I asked.

"No," Katori replied. "This is it."

Domori used his torch to light sconces affixed to the walls. The flames illuminated two decorative bronze doors. Each one had a giant wingless dragon emblazoned on it, the beasts facing one another.

"The guardians of *Ho-musubi,*" Katori said,

kneeling before the doors. "The Terran god of fire."

Domori and Haruna also knelt, whispering a prayer. I remained where I was and kept quiet out of respect, though I wondered about the temple itself. Who had built it? And why was it underground? So many questions, as Katori had said.

All three of them rose, and Katori removed an amulet from around her neck. It was small, no bigger than a coin, and circular, forged of silver with a ruby in the center. The amulet was attached to a thin silver chain. Aside from its ability to remove the wards on the temple doors, it was also pretty to look at.

"Prepare yourselves," Katori said. "We do not know what lies on the other side."

Domori and Haruna drew their swords and took up positions on either side of her. I rested my hand on the hilt of my blade and looked at Sion. She watched the doors curiously.

Do you sense anything? I asked.

Nothing, she replied. *The wards are powerful. They're blocking everything.*

Let's hope the enenra isn't real.

We shall see soon enough.

Katori pressed the amulet into a space that rested along the crevice of the doors. The ruby flashed briefly, and a grinding sound filled the tunnel.

"What is that?" I asked.

"The locking mechanism. From what I understand, it is retreating into the walls to allow the doors to open."

The grinding stopped and Katori removed the amulet, placing it back around her neck. She slipped her fingers into the space where the amulet had been and pulled. The doors creaked open and there was nothing but darkness. Katori looked back at me, and I nodded at her.

Together, we stepped into oblivion.

THE END OF BOOK EIGHT

ABOUT THE AUTHOR

Richard Fierce is a fantasy and space opera author. He's been writing since childhood, but began publishing in 2007. Since then, he's written multiple novels and short stories.

In 2000, Richard won Poet of the Year for his poem *The Darkness*. He's also one of the creative brains behind the Allatoona Book Festival, a literary event in Acworth, Georgia.

A recovering retail worker, he now works in the tech industry when he's not busy writing.

He's married and has three step-daughters (pray for him), three dogs (two huskies!), three cats, two ferrets and a fish. He basically has a zoo.

His love affair with fantasy was born in high school when a friend's mother gave him a copy of *Dragons of Spring Dawning* by Margaret Weis and Tracy Hickman.

www.ingramcontent.com/pod-product-compliance
Lightning Source LLC
Chambersburg PA
CBHW032040180726

48284CB00008B/2673